Sangeet and the MISSING BEAT

KIRANJOT KAUR

"For KNK and BNK, from
Mom, with love."

Rebel Mountain Press

Sangeet loves music.
She can play five different
instruments and she can sing, too.
She is always composing something
new and telling everyone about her
musical tunes and rhythms.

Her favourite instrument is the tabla.
The tabla is handmade and each player who plays it makes their
own unique sounds. It is amazing. Sangeet has seen many men, and
a few women, play tabla—but of course, anyone can do anything!
Someday, Sangeet is going to be a tabla master.

One day, after school, Sangeet had exciting news. "Dad, Dad, Dad!!
The most super-duper, best thing *ever* happened at recess today!"

"There were noises everywhere—the teeter-totter was bouncing, the swings were squeaking, and all the kids were laughing and screaming. Then, through it all, I heard the most incredible beat in my head! It's perfect for my tabla! I'll play it now so you can hear it, too."

Sangeet's dad smiled and raced her to her room.

Sangeet sat down criss-crossed at her tabla.

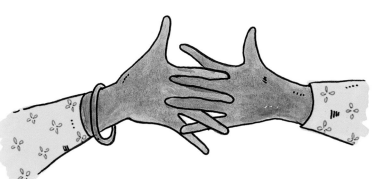

She flexed her fingers and gave her wrists a good shake.

Then she took a deep breath, straightened her posture, and began to play.

Dhin Dhin DaGeh ThitKita
She tried it again.
Dhin Dhin DaGeh ThitKita
Hmmm. Still not quite right.

She looked at her dad in confusion.

"Dad, I've got half a beat stuck in my head and there's something missing. What am I going to do; what am I going to *doooo*?"

"I'm sure you'll figure it out. You always do," Sangeet's dad replied with confidence.

Sangeet shrugged and continued to practise playing her beat.

She played for hours and then after dinner, she played again
until bedtime, trying to get it right. When Sangeet's mom
came to say goodnight, Sangeet was playing pretend
tabla with her hands on her thighs.

"What are you working on, Sangeet?" asked her mom.

"Mom! I've got a half beat stuck in my head and something is missing."

"How about if you try again tomorrow? I'm sure you'll figure it out. You always do." Sangeet's mom smiled and tucked her into bed.

That night, Sangeet dreamed of her completed beat.

It played through the skies among the clouds, through the forests and across the rivers in beautiful, timeless ripples. The mountains of rock, the little blades of grass, and all the creatures vibrated with the same beat.

The next morning, Sangeet tried to recreate the beat from her dream.
Dhin Dhin DaGeh ThitKita
It still wasn't right!
But Sangeet wouldn't give up.
She drummed her pencil during class.

She played tabla on her lap at recess,

and she even tapped her feet while she ate.

By the end of the week, Sangeet was out of ideas and feeling a little discouraged.

"Sangeet!" called her mom. "Look who's here!"

"Dadiji!" Sangeet jumped into her grandma's arms. Sangeet's grandma was a musical genius. She had travelled the world playing music of all kinds. She'd know what to do with her unfinished beat!

"Dadiji! Dadiji! I need your help!
I've got half a beat stuck in my head and I can't figure out
the rest. What should I do; what should I *doooo*?"
"Let's hear it!" Sangeet's grandma said, excitedly.

"Sangeet played her beat for her grandma who smiled as she listened.
Dhin Dhin DaGeh ThitKita

"See? Something is missing. What can I do?"

Sangeet's grandma paused to think before answering.

"Every great musician knows that you need to practise and also listen."

"Listen?" asked Sangeet. "But I hear the beat all the time in my head and I still can't get it right."

"Sangeet," said her grandma, "I'm sure you'll figure it out. You always do."

Sangeet knew her grandma had to be right, but she still didn't know what to do. She thought about when she first heard the beat. It all started with a sound. She needed to listen. What could she listen to? It was quiet now except for noises from the kitchen.

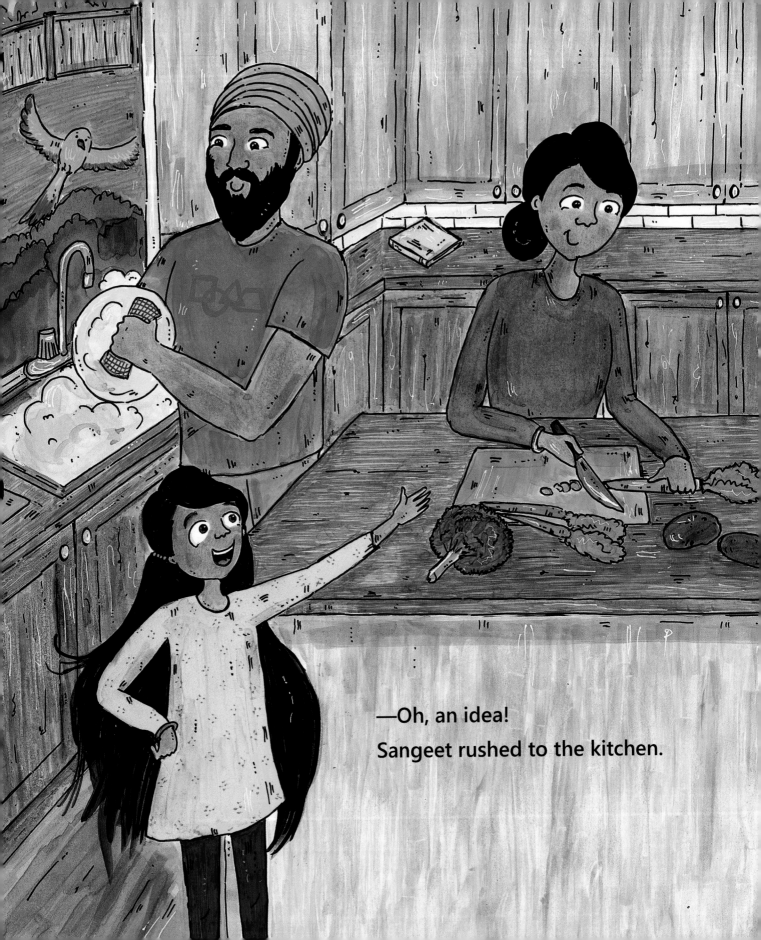

—Oh, an idea!
Sangeet rushed to the kitchen.

"Everybody! I need your help! I've got half a beat stuck in my head and I think I might know what to do to finish it!"

"Dad, I need you to . . . do the dishes.

Mom, I need you to . . . chop some veggies and . . .

. . . tap your feet. And . . .

. . . yes! Dadiji, can you sit on this stool and . . . tap your spoon on the table?" Sangeet instructed everyone to create overlapping sounds.

She closed her eyes and listened as her beat emerged from among the sounds around her.

Dhin Dhin DaGeh ThitKita
Tu Na Ka Tha
DaGeh ThitKita
Dhin Na

There it was!

"I've got it!!" Sangeet played the completed beat on her tabla for everyone to hear. They nodded their heads as they took in the sounds. Everyone loved it as much as Sangeet.

When her grandma said goodbye, she gave Sangeet a big hug and said, "I knew you could do it! You really have an ear for music. I can't wait to hear what you come up with next!"

Sangeet listened to her grandma's footsteps tap on the walkway. The way her grandma moved made a beautiful rhythm that would be perfect on her tabla! Sangeet ran to her tabla and got to work composing a new, fantastic beat.

Glossary:

- tabla: twin percussion instrument, thought to have originated from the Indian subcontinent.
- dadiji: from dadi, a paternal grandmother. "ji" is a term of respect often attached to the names of relations.
- Sangeet: a name which means "music"

ALL ABOUT THE AUTHOR AND ILLUSTRATOR

Kiranjot Kaur is a multi-disciplinary artist, author, and engineer. Her work aims to celebrate her artistic influences including her Panjabi, Sikh, and Canadian heritages. Kiranjot's goal in developing children's books is to create stories and art representative of her life growing up in B.C.'s Lower Mainland, and she hopes to inspire kids to dream big and recognize their own amazing potential (just like Sangeet!).

Among many artistic adventures, Kiranjot is currently pursuing a PhD in earthquake engineering. She lives with her two incredible daughters and loving husband in Surrey, B.C., Canada.

Sangeet and the Missing Beat
Published by Rebel Mountain Press, 2022

Text and Illustrations copyright © 2022 by Kiranjot Kaur

Author photograph, by Jeremy Lim
Acknowledgment and thanks to Gurmukh Singh Aujla
for his assistance with tabla and music content.

Library and Archives Canada Cataloguing in Publication

Title: Sangeet and the missing beat / written and illustrated by Kiranjot Kaur.
Names: Kaur, Kiranjot, author, illustrator.
Identifiers: Canadiana 20210229896 | ISBN 9781989996058 (softcover)
Classification: LCC PS8621.A6925 S26 2022 | DDC jC813/.6—dc23

Rebel Mountain Press gratefully acknowledges project support by the Province of British Columbia through the BC Arts Council.

Supported by the Province of British Columbia

Printed and bound in Canada
ISBN 978-1-989996-05-8

Rebel Mountain Press—Nanoose Bay, BC, Canada
We gratefully acknowledge that we are located on the traditional territory of the Snaw-Naw-As First Nation

www.rebelmountainpress.com

CHILDREN'S PICTURE BOOKS from REBEL MOUNTAIN PRESS

by Sunita Pal, Illustrated by Cody Andreasen
978-1-9992416-0-5 HC $19.95 Ages 3-8

Cancer is a C Word will help families and schools introduce the concept of cancer to young children in a very simple and gentle way that is easy for them to understand. Cancer is a C Word also reminds children of other stronger C words that can help someone affected by cancer, such as caring, cuddling, compassion and community.

"This gentle educational primer on a tough topic pushes through fear and lands on love." **~Kirkus Reviews**

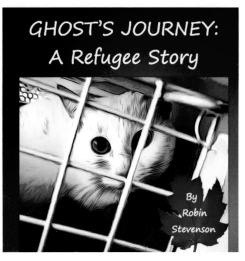

by Robin Stevenson, Illustrated by Rainer Oktovianus
978-1-7753019-4-3 HC Ages 4-10

When life in Indonesia becomes too dangerous for LGBTQ people, Ghost and her two dads are forced to leave their home and escape to freedom in Canada. Based on a true story, and told from the perspective of the real-life cat, Ghost.

"This introduction to LGBTQ human rights for young children is a gentle and effective one." **~Kirkus Reviews**

"Stevenson's picture book manages to present this complicated subject in an accessible and moving way." **~Quill and Quire**

Award Nominations: 2021 Silver Birch Express, and 2021 Rocky Mountain Book Award

by Gail Marlene Schwartz & Lucie Gagnon, Illustrated by Amélie Ayotte
978-1-989996-03-4 HC $19.95 Ages 4-8

Samuel knows that their real name is Simone, but things at their house are too quiet to think about how to tell their parents. When Chloe the costume designer moves in across the street with a dog about to have puppies, life becomes bigger, more colourful, and louder. And so does Simone.

"With the support of a caring babysitter, a child longing for connection and self-expression fulfills their dream of owning a puppy. A sweet and upbeat celebration." **~Kirkus Reviews**

French-language version also available- **Quels jappements!**
by Lucie Gagnon and Gail Marlene Schwartz; 978-1-989996-04-1